D1264167

# ESCAPE FROM PLANET ALCATRAZ

# ATTACK OF THE DRONES

BY MICHAEL DAHL

ILLUSTRATED BY PATRICIO CLAREY

STONE ARCH BOOKS
a capstone imprint

Escape from Planet Alcatraz is published by
Stone Arch Books
A Capstone Imprint
1710 Roe Crest Drive
North Mankato, Minnesota 56003
www.capstonepub.com

Library of Congress Cataloging-in-Publication Data
Names: Dahl, Michael, author. | Clarey, Patricio, 1978– illustrator.
Title: Attack of the drones / by Michael Dahl ; illustrated by
    Patricio Clarey.
Description: North Mankato, MN : Stone Arch Books, a Capstone
    imprint, [2020] | Series: Escape from planet Alcatraz
Identifiers: LCCN 2019005604 (print) | LCCN 2019007543 (ebook) |
    ISBN 9781496583222 (eBook PDF) | ISBN 9781496583154
    (library binding)
Subjects: LCSH: Science fiction. | Prisons—Juvenile fiction. | Escapes—
    Juvenile fiction. | Extraterrestrial beings—Juvenile fiction. | Drone
    aircraft—Juvenile fiction. | Extrasolar planets—Juvenile fiction. |
    Stowaways—Juvenile fiction. | Adventure stories. | CYAC: Science
    fiction. | Prisons—Fiction. | Escapes—Fiction. | Extraterrestrial
    beings—Fiction. | Drone aircraft—Fiction. | Stowaways—Fiction. |
    Adventure and adventurers—Fiction. | LCGFT: Science fiction. |
    Action and adventure fiction.
Classification: LCC PZ7.D15134 (ebook) | LCC PZ7.D15134
    At 2020 (print) | DDC 813.54 [Fic]—dc23
LC record available at https://lccn.loc.gov/2019005604

Summary: Zak Nine and his alien friend, Erro, are trying to escape the
prison planet known as Alcatraz. The boys are currently hiding out in
the planet's Scarlet Jungle. But they aren't out of danger yet. It's bad
enough that they are being chased by the prison's killer drones. But the
jungle itself is full of creatures that are almost as deadly!

Editor: Aaron J. Sautter
Designer: Kay Fraser
Production Specialist: Katy LaVigne

Design elements: Shutterstock: Agustina Camilion, A-Star, Dima Zel,
Draw_Wing_Zen, Hybrid_Graphics, Metallic Citizen

Printed and bound in the United States of America.
PA71

# TABLE OF CONTENTS

ERRO

PLATEAU of LENG

PHANTOM FOREST

POISON SEA

VULCAN MOUNTAINS

LAKE of GOLD

METAL MOON

DIAMOND MINES

MONSTER ZOO

PITS OF NO RETURN

PRISON STRONGHOLDS

SWAMP OF FLAME

SCARLET JUNGLE

PRISON ENERGY DRIVES

SPACE PORT PRISONER INTAKE

ABYSS OF GIANTS

ZAK

# THE PRISONERS

## ZAK NINE

Zak is a teenage boy from Earth Base Zeta. He dreams of piloting a star fighter one day. Zak is very brave and is a quick thinker. But his enthusiasm often leads him into trouble.

## ERRO

Erro is a teenage furling from the planet Quom. He has the fur, long tail, sharp eyes, and claws of his species. Erro is often impatient with Zak's reckless ways. But he shares his friend's love of adventure.

# THE PRISON PLANET

*Alcatraz* . . . there is no escape from this terrifying prison planet. It's filled with dungeons, traps, endless deserts, and other dangers. Zak Nine and his alien friend, Erro, are trapped here. They had sneaked onto a ship hoping to see an awesome space battle. But the ship landed on Alcatraz instead. Now they have to work together if they ever hope to escape!

## ERRO'S STORY . . . A JUNGLE HIDEOUT >>>

Zak and I are hiding from Alcatraz's robot guards in a thick, red jungle. The robots cannot follow us here. But we keep hearing many strange sounds. Zak thinks the guards are using attack drones to hunt us down. If that is true, it will not be long before they find us. . . . >>>>

# CHAPTER ONE:
## BUZZ!

This red jungle is endless. Zak and I have been hiding here for several days. Luckily the Alcatraz guards cannot follow us through the thick trees.

But there is still danger here. We have not seen any creatures in the jungle, but we can hear them. At night we hear weird bird cries in the dark.

At night we take turns sleeping. We only sleep a few hours before we start moving again.

# BZZZZZ!

Huge horned insects fly among the jungle's giant flowers. The buzzing bugs are almost as big as us.

I point them out to Zak. "They look like your Earth buzz," I say.

"You mean *bees*," says Zak. "*Buzz* is the sound they make."

*Bees? Buzz? What is the difference?* I think.

"Your language is tricky," I say.

We watch the noisy insects flit among the big, bell-shaped flowers.

"Watch out for their stingers," says Zak. "They're huge!"

**ZZZZZZZZ!**

We hear another buzzing sound overhead. But this sound does not come from the insects. It comes from high above the trees.

"Robot guards?" I ask.

"No—drones!" Zak shouts.

## CHAPTER TWO:
# UNDERFOOT

We run deeper into the jungle.
The trees' thick, red leaves crowd
out the light.

**ZZZZZZZ!**

"They are getting closer!" I warn.

I start running faster. The last
time drones chased us, they fired
lasers. I do not like laser blasters.

"Oooohhhhhh!" Zak cries out behind me.

I run back to find Zak lying on the ground. His eyes are shut tight with pain.

"Did a laser hit you?" I ask. "I do not see any drones."

"My foot!" groans Zak.

"The laser hit your foot?"

"No!" he says. "My foot caught on a stupid root, and I fell."

Zak rubs his ankle. "I don't think I can run on it," he says.

Zak always sounds brave, but this time I see fear in his eyes.

"I can help," I say. "Hold on to my shoulder."

Zak shakes his head. "No. I'll only slow you down," he says.

The leaves suddenly start shaking overhead.

*Oh no!* I think. *The drones are here!*

## CHAPTER THREE:
# UNDER ATTACK!

But it is not the drones. Hundreds of screeching, colorful birds suddenly drop from the branches above us. Then they fly deeper into the jungle.

"That is not normal," I tell Zak. "Something must have scared them."

Bright lights flash between the leaves above us.

# KRRROOOOOSH!

A powerful laser beam hits the branch above us, and it bursts into flame.

"You were right," says Zak.
"The drones scared the birds. We
have to keep moving!"

Zak holds on to my shoulder as
we move through the trees.

"Many creatures live in this jungle," I tell my friend. "That should help fool the drones' sensors."

"Maybe. But few creatures can walk on two legs like us," Zak says.

"Then we have to hide our legs,"
I reply.

Zak snorts. "Right. Are you some sort
of magician, fur boy?"

My Quom eyes can see a large shape
ahead of us.

"No, Earth boy," I say. "But I grew
up in a jungle like this. I know how
things work."

**ZZZZZZAAAATT!**

Another laser blast barely misses us.

"Yeah? Well I know how lasers work," Zak replies. "Trust me, you don't want to find out."

We hide in the shadow of a large tree. Zak leans against the trunk.

Now he sees the same large shape that I do.

It is a large lake. Far out on the lake sits a huge flock of the colorful birds.

# CHAPTER FOUR:
## UNDER WATER

The tree suddenly shakes violently.

**KRASSSH!**

A burning branch falls next to us.

"Look!" Zak points at two shapes flying above us.

The drones have shiny metal bodies and short wings. Red and orange lights blink at both ends.

They remind me of the buzzing insects we saw before.

"Come on!" I yell, pulling Zak into the lake with me. "The water will hide us."

"We can't hide down there forever," says Zak. "We need to breathe!"

I look around and see more big, bell-like flowers growing by the water. I grab two of them and hand one to Zak.

"Quick! Put this over your head," I tell him.

We slip the flowers over our heads and stumble into the lake.

The large blossoms hold pockets of air. We can breathe as we sink deeper into the water.

"It's like a diving helmet!" says Zak.

"Yes, just breathe normally and keep swimming," I tell him.

## CHAPTER FIVE:
# FLIGHT OF FREEDOM

I pull Zak deeper into the lake.

**ZHHHOOOOM!**

More lasers slice through the water nearby. I feel warm bubbles swirling around me.

*Just a little farther,* I tell myself.
*We need to get close to those alien birds.*

The birds may be like the ones on Quom. When one flies, the others follow.

Then I hear a strange noise from under the water. It is the muffled roar of a thousand screaming birds. I swim up to the surface to see more.

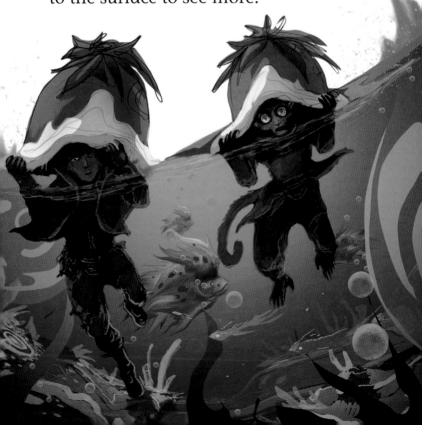

The huge flock of alien birds rises into the sky. It swarms past the drones, confusing them. Dozens of the panicking birds crash into the buzzing aircraft.

Zak's head bobs up next to mine. We both watch as the damaged drones fall into the lake with a splash.

"That was awesome!" says Zak.

We both take a gulp of air and dive underwater with our flower helmets. We continue swimming toward the other side of the lake.

If we are lucky, we can escape before more deadly drones arrive. . . .

# GLOSSARY

**diving helmet** (DYV-ing HEL-muht)—a large, round helmet worn over the head; usually used to supply air for a deep-sea diver

**drone** (DROHN)—an unmanned aircraft that is controlled from the ground

**dungeon** (DUHN-juhn)—a prison, usually underground

**flit** (FLIT)—to move lightly and quickly

**jungle** (JUHNG-guhl)—land thickly covered with trees, vines, and bushes

**laser** (LAY-zur)—a thin, intense beam of light

**panicking** (PAN-ik-ing)—to be in a state of extreme fear or terror

**sensor** (SEN-sur)—a device that can detect changes in the environment

**species** (SPEE-sheez)—a group of living things that share similar features

**stinger** (STING-ur)—a sharp, pointy part of an animal that can be used to sting

# TALK ABOUT IT

1. At the start of the story, Erro and Zak are taking turns sleeping as they hide from the Alcatraz guards. Do you think this is a wise choice? Explain your answer.

2. Erro confused the word "buzz" with the word "bees" in the story. Have you confused words with others that sound similar? Share some examples of words you think are confusing.

3. Erro wanted to run, but helped support Zak after he hurt his ankle. Talk about a time when you helped a friend in need, even though you might have wanted to do something else instead.

# WRITE ABOUT IT

1. Many strange creatures live in planet Alcatraz's Scarlet Jungle. Use your imagination to create a list of creatures that might live there. Write a brief description for each.

2. Can you think of another way Zak and Erro could escape from the deadly drones? Write a new ending to the story using your own plans for the boys to escape.

# ABOUT THE AUTHOR

Michael Dahl is the author of more than 300 books for young readers, including the bestselling Library of Doom series. He is a huge fan of Star Trek, Star Wars, and Doctor Who. He has a fear of closed-in spaces, but has visited several prisons, dungeons, and strongholds, both ancient and modern. He made a daring escape from each one. Luckily, the guards still haven't found him.

# ABOUT THE ILLUSTRATOR

Patricio Clarey was born in 1978 in Argentina. He graduated in fine arts at the School of Visual Arts Martín Malharro, specializing in illustration and graphic design. Patricio currently lives in Barcelona, Spain, where he works as a freelance graphic designer and illustrator. He has created several comics and graphic novels, and his work has been featured in several books and other publications. Patricio is working on launching his first art book, *Attractor.*